"WHO ARE YOU?"

"WHO ARE YOU?"

by John Schindel

Illustrated by James Watts

MARGARET K. McELDERRY BOOKS
NEW YORK

Collier Macmillan Canada
TORONTO

Maxwell Macmillan International Publishing Group
NEW YORK   OXFORD   SINGAPORE   SYDNEY

Margaret K. McElderry Books
Macmillan Publishing Company
866 Third Avenue
New York, NY 10022

Collier Macmillan Canada, Inc.
1200 Eglinton Avenue East
Suite 200
Don Mills, Ontario M3C 3N1

First edition
Printed in Hong Kong
10 9 8 7 6 5 4 3 2 1

Library of Congress Cataloging-in-Publication Data
Schindel, John.
"Who are you?" / John Schindel ; illustrated by James Watts.
p.   cm.
Summary: When Brown Bear's parents tell him that he is too small
to attend the party they are giving, he dresses up in their clothes
and arrives as a mysterious guest whom no one knows.
ISBN 0–689–50523–X
[1. Parties—Fiction. 2. Bears—Fiction.] I. Watts, James,
1955– ill. II. Title.
PZ7.S346328Wh 1991
[E]—dc20
90-39850
CIP
AC

For Ellen; for Mort
J. S.

For Julian
J. W.

"May I come to your party tonight?" asked
Brown Bear.

"No," said his parents, "you are too small."

"I will stand on a chair the whole time,"
said Brown Bear. "Then I will not be so
small."

"Standing on a chair might make you taller," said his mother, "but you are still too little."

"I will stand on a chair with pillows
stuffed under my shirt," said Brown Bear.
"Then I will be taller and bigger."

"Pillows might make you bigger," said
his father, "but you are still too young.
That is why you cannot come."

"I will stand on a chair with pillows under my shirt and hold up a sign that says I am two hundred years old," said Brown Bear. "Then I will be taller and bigger and older than everyone."

"No, Brown Bear," replied his parents.
"Tonight's party is only for grown-ups."

After the grown-ups had arrived, Brown Bear hid in the hall closet and carefully watched what they did.

Then he quietly crept closer and listened from behind a chair. Being a grown-up seems easy, he thought.

Then Brown Bear had an idea!
He tiptoed into his parents' bedroom.

First he put on his father's emerald green
tuxedo. It was too big, but Brown Bear did
not mind. It made him feel grown-up.

Then he tied a pink scarf around his
neck. It was too long, but Brown Bear did
not mind. It made him feel important.
    But something is missing, he thought,
because I still look like me.

He cut out a paper mustache. It was lopsided, but Brown Bear did not mind. It made him feel wise.

Then he tried on his mother's straw hat,
but its flowers made Brown Bear feel silly.

Next he tried on a sombrero, but it was
too floppy and round.

Then he put on a shiny top hat, which
made him feel taller and bigger and older,
just as he knew he should be.

Brown Bear was pleased with his disguise.

If I can't tell that I am me, thought
Brown Bear, then nobody can. So nobody
will know it's me!

He sneaked out the back door, hurried
around the house, and knock-knock-knocked
loudly on the front door.

Brown Bear's father opened the door.

"How are you, Mr. Bear?" asked
Brown Bear in a deep, muffled voice.

"Fine, thank you," replied Mr. Bear.
"But who are you?"

At first Brown Bear did not know what
to say or who he should be, and he was scared.

"I am Brown Bear Doctor," he said, and
then he quickly said, "Doctor," once again.

Poor Brown Bear. He was very
confused, but he tried again.

"I am Brown Bear's doctor Doctor
Doctor. I fix Brown Bear when he is sick."

"Oh! It is a pleasure to meet you,
Doctor Doctor," said Mr. Bear. "May I
take your hat?"

"Why do you want my hat?" asked
Brown Bear. "Don't *you* have any hats?"

"Yes, of course I do," replied Mr. Bear.
"I even have one just like yours!"

"Then you do not need mine!" said
Brown Bear, and with that, he shuffled
inside, coattails and pant legs sweeping the
floor behind him.

Brown Bear mixed and mingled among
the guests, but no one seemed to notice him.

He nibbled mysterious vegetables and
gooey cheeses. One tasted worse than
another.

And when Brown Bear reached for the
punch, his sleeve swished into the flower
vase and toppled it over.

Then one of the guests told a funny
story. Everyone burst out laughing, except
Brown Bear. He didn't understand it at all.

"I wish I was playing with my SpaceBear
game or watching TV," he muttered.

"Hello, sir," said his mother. "Are you
having a good time?"

"No," said Brown Bear, "I am not."

"Would you like to dance with me?"
asked his mother.

"Yes," said Brown Bear, "I would."

Brown Bear's mother picked him up.
They swirled and twirled around the room.

"Now I am having fun!" said Brown
Bear. But it ended all too soon.

Everyone applauded. Brown Bear
took a bow.
"I have had a very nice dance," said
Brown Bear's mother, "but it's nearly
time for bed."

"It's too early for you to go to bed,"
said Brown Bear.

"Yes," replied Mrs. Bear, "it is too early
for me, but not for my Brown Bear."

"Brown Bear is good," said Brown
Bear. "He must be in his pajamas by now."

"I should go then and tell him a story,"
said his mother. "He likes bedtime stories,
you know."

"Oh, so do I!" said Brown Bear. "I will go and tell him one for you."

"Thank you," said Mrs. Bear. "That is very kind. Now I can stay at the party."

Brown Bear filled his hat with chocolate-chip cookies in case he got hungry during the night.

"Good night," said Mrs. Bear. "I hope you will come again."

Brown Bear felt very proud and hurried off to bed.

I acted grown-up, thought Brown Bear,
even if I'm not old or big or tall.

But being grown-up wasn't much fun.
It's more fun being me!